The
Teacher's
Dream
Fulfilled

The
Teacher's
Dream
Fulfilled

J. Fern

authorHOUSE®

AuthorHouse™
1663 Liberty Drive
Bloomington, IN 47403
www.authorhouse.com
Phone: 1-800-839-8640

Published by AuthorHouse   05/29/2013

ISBN: 978-1-4817-4982-4 (sc)
ISBN: 978-1-4817-4981-7 (e)

Library of Congress Control Number: 2013908340

Any people depicted in stock imagery provided by Thinkstock are models, and such images are being used for illustrative purposes only.
Certain stock imagery © Thinkstock.

This book is printed on acid-free paper.

Bob was graduating with some masters degree and lived in N.Y.C. He was not keen of staying teaching in the city was from a small family.

Two child families. He always traveled was fond of small towns. He remembered one in his travels that stuck with him one he liked.

A town located in Iowa that he could live and teach history he was a buff. He told his parents and sister that he was moving there. Leaving Tuesday.

They wished him well then all hugged each other. Tuesday came, and he kissed them goodbye. He had a new car given to him by parents on graduating. He would take his time three days.

To get there, He was glad to see the town, reminded him of movies that he saw a small town where everybody knows you. He was now looking for a hotel.

He found one and settled in. The local paper he picked up in hotel he looked at and saw That was a new high school just finished being built, they were interviewing teachers.

He dressed up went to the interview. Bob was just 23 good looking was hoping. His turn came he had a masters degree in history. They asked why not teach in N.Y. He said I had enough of the big city life. When I traveled I came across your little town. I knew I would like to live and teach here being a history buff I can explore this area. I feel strong about that hope you can use a history teacher.

Well they said are you set up in town. Bob said yes at a hotel locally and will be looking for a home to buy.

I just need to see what is available. They told him school starts in two weeks the teachers we hire will be there this week to get their rooms started. Any problem with that. Bob said no eager to start. Well young man you are hired as our first history teacher congratulations. Bob said thank you I will make you proud. They gave him papers To sign and gave him address of school who to see.

Bob felt good about being hired went back to his hotel. He had a refrigerator, microwave stocked with food perfect for awhile. Bob left since he was a history buff he read His map about places of interest. He saw a covered bridge 100 years old. He went there He saw a covered bridge 100 years old just something a history buff would be interested in.

Looked saw a local library stopped went in asked lot of questions to nice lady. Looked around for books that would interest him. Joined the library. Took out three books. It was 4:30pm he thought to get back to hotel to read take it easy.

At 10:30pm he went to bed he got up at 6am made something to eat. It was only half hour to school not to bad. He parked saw a beautiful setting trees embraced school just perfect.

He went to front door opened it went in he could smell the newness. He was in a good mood went through hallway saw office open. Bob went in a women was there he told her he was a history teacher she got up said come with me she took him to his room said good luck.

Bob said thank you went in the desk were set up there were thirty he counted. Stayed there till 3pm then left to look for a sales book of homes for sale. In the book bob was looking for a small home to start. There were several that looked interesting.

He thought that before he starts teaching, that he would get a home, Bob planned the next day to look. Next day looked at five homes liked one of them It was a two bedroom two bath home. The owners were very nice.

When bob told them he was a teacher just hired by new high school they told him they were teachers too. Bob was given the tour of home they asked where are you from. Bob told them in his travels he saw this town it stayed in his head when he graduated he told his family.

He loved what he saw he had enough of the big city life. That why I am here to teach. How about a cup of tea some crackers Bob said fine. They talked about what he taught. Bob said history I am a history buff will teach at the new beautiful high school.

They said the new high school on Adams street Bob said yes. Well they said we are teachers as well for 30 years that is why we are moving to florida. Bob asked what did you teach. They said we both were math teachers at the old school. Bob said that is something else. They asked do you like our home. Bob said I love it. They talked about the price gave Bob 5,000 off.

Bob was so taken by them they were hugging each other before Bob left. They told him you will not have to worry about this home we replaced everything. Bob told them if they visit this place stay with me. the next day they went to a lawyer they knew he drew up contract for sale Bob signed gave deposit of 500 to seal the deal. The lawyer asked when is closing before school starts Bob told him should have a mortgage by then, went to bank to apply was told should have it in two weeks. So everything was in place Bob was excited about the home how fast everything is coming into place. Bob was also enthused about the People he met what a coincidence they were teachers. Bob also thought about there furniture Thought he would have to go to stores replace them. Furniture was old he thought I will. Go to the mall to sears buy new furniture. The people are leaving a lot but at 23 I just Want my own style. The next day Bob got up early went to sears saw bought furniture.

He also bought new refrigerator, stove, tv 42 inch. Put it all on pay as you go date of delivery. He went to hotel and rested the next day he went to school to see what was going on.

When he got there was a lot going on saw a lot of teachers were there. He met one guy that teaches math told him about the home he just bought they were math teachers.

He knew the people said great folks Bob agreed said they are moving to florida. My name is Matthew Slovak what is your name Bob Evans I teach history. Well good luck with first class.

Bob said one more week school opens. All the kids will come Bob thought they cannot be bad as N.Y.C. Then left to the hotel thinking of all he has accomplished this week he was amazed.
Bob put on some food in the microwave. When finished he ate watched tv till 10pm. Then Went to sleep. The next day again back to school, the auditorium was big, saw where they ate.

Went out side to the rear and saw a baseball field thought about it for extra money. Bob went to the gym asked about the position they asked what his background was. Bob said I know the game played ball in N.Y. I know I can coach baseball. They asked if he thought he could be head coach.

Bob said yes no problem. The gym coach made Bob the head coach told the office said it is your baby so take it from here. Bob went to the office asked them to put something in the news bulletin about trying out for baseball team. Bob made a sign put on the concession wall for tryouts.

Bob then went back to office told them about the sign in case anyone sees it and call. Bob went Back to hotel about 4pm put something in microwave to eat. Bob started to think what his baseball Team needs he knew first pitching stops hitting. Bob first action to find pitching while others tryout.

The next day at school he asked the gym teacher who do we play. We play the high schools from 50 miles away all others. The next day at the office if we have a baseball team who do we play. They said you will play in 50 mile area the high schools. There are 15 of them there are 30 games a year.

Bob thought about that we will need a bus to travel. Bob went to gym asked gym teacher asked him about a bus said we have to look for one. that afternoon Ed told Bob lets go in my car I live here know people. They went about 25 miles away to a graveyard of cars and buses.

The owner knew Ed. Who told him that we are starting a baseball team that will play high schools 50 mile area can you recommend something in a bus for us. He said Ed I will find the best bus here put new tires on it, paint it, fix the motor giving it back to the school system. Ed said thank you It will be ready in a week. He said. Bob thought that Ed knew the guy and he came through.

They went back to the school Bob went home put something in microwave to eat. Bob thought watching tv news what a difference in news broadcasting from N.Y.

Bob put on a movie watched it till 10pm felt tired went to bed with a book The next day was interesting, teachers together in auditorium the principle miss. Cummings gave her speech on what she expected of us. When that was over I went to my room looked at text they gave me to teach. I was comfortable with it knew I could put some interest to it.

There was two more days to week Monday starets school. I left at 3pm went to hotel. Friday I will go to bank to see about mortgage. They said it was approved would get it Monday. He called the lawyer said Monday we can close I got my mortgage. They set closing for 3pm.

All were there Monday at 3pm were glad to see each other. They asked Bob how was your first day. Bob said normal as much as I expected. The closing took place and they took Bob out to eat. Bob said to them have a safe trip to Florida. Hope to see you again. Bob had the keys to home they started their trip to florida. Bob went to finalize hotel then left to home. when he got there he looked out back at the yard. Saw it was big with a few fruit trees.

Bob thought it is big enough for a pool someday. Bob called electric co. the telephone co.

They said they would be there the next day. Bob new that sears would deliver also. he looked to see where he would sleep make office of other room. The bell rang he went to door and it was sears with the furniture. They hooked up took everything away.

Bob thought to paint the kitchen would do it nights after school and weekends. He filled his refrigerator with soda beer, had some cold cuts needed to get butter. The phone was working The tv is great with cable connected. The new 42 inch was a pleasure to watch. The cable was working fine. All the comforts of home. Bob heard the phone ring went to answer it was a young, man who saw his baseball sign told him see me in gym class at 12 noon. The next day at 12 pm Bob went to the gym to meet the guy. When he saw the guy was 6ft 4 inches 230 lbs. Bob said You are a big boy any baseball experience at all. This guy never played before but was athletic.

Bob was thinking right hand pitcher may be. Bob told him to come to baseball field at 4pmI want to show you what I have in mind. At the field the young man came brought a glove. Bob said nice glove

Bob put on his glove said to the young man to lets have a catch. He threw a heavy ball Bob thought he is our right hand pitcher. The next day at the baseball field fifteen guys showed up. Bob thought

Real nice once we have the position filled almost a team. The catcher was 6ft 200 lp. Bob spoke with the catcher wanted him to catch the young man continually. Told the catcher I will teach him pitching the baseball how to use the plate. After selecting his infield, outfield he needed more pitchers.

But felt the team was coming together. He had what a team in his mind should look like was very up on his getting the players he has. The right hand was taking to pitching was throwing hard about 89 to 93. He had smarts too taking my advice had control I was pleased with his pitching.

I had him through batting practice but I told him throw easy let them hit it. On any given day you would strike them out. He understood we got hitting in but need more pitchers. The next day in class

Anyone in here played baseball a couple hands went up I asked what position one said pitcher I asked where he said growing up in Maryland I pitched for a team 3 YEARS. Bob asked I invite you to come to the field and try out. Ok class today we get to learn about how big Rome got and how it got destroyed it will take all semester to go through and you will know the history.

Bob was in the hallway when he heard hello there. He turned around a pretty young girl saying hello the girl said you bought a house from friends of mine. they were great to me

Bob said. She said my name is Caitlin Summers, they told me to get to know you because you were very special. Well that was nice of them to say that. Bob asked are you a teacher here yes she said I teach Physical Education. That is a good course, I teach history class you can call me a history buff. Well I love what I teach as well she said. Bob said when you love what your doing it is the best work. Bob asked if he could get with her again I have to teach class in 5 minutes. Caitlin said sure what day is good for you. Bob thought being busy with baseball now a girl. She sure is pretty nice he said Saturday night. Caitlin said what time Bob said 6pm.

Caitlin said I will be at your home at 6pm. Bob said ok left to class, when he saw the faces sitting there, he thought waiting to learn. Class open your books to page 10 and follow me. By the way did any of you play baseball. Two hands went up when bob asked., Both played one pitched.

Come to the field after school I will look at what you can do. Bob said Today we are going to talk about the Roman Empire how big it got, how amazing it got. We will start on page 10 history book.

The bell rang at 3pm as the class was leaving Bob said to the two guys bring your gloves also at 4pm.

At 4pm Bob was at the field when the two boys came with their gloves. To the pitcher he said go on the mound warm up with a few throws before we start. Bob went behind the plate caught the pitches. After awhile Bob said you can start throwing now. Bob said no curves

After about twenty pitches Bob saw evidence that this kid had control and threw very well.

Bob said we practice on Saturday here can you come. The boy said yes thank you. The other boy played the outfield was a big kid 6ft 160 lbs. Bob said go to left I will hit you some balls. After that Bob said get up and I will throw you some pitches. Bob saw he can catch was interested if he could hit. When batting came Bob threw him twenty pitches the kid smacked two over the left field fence Bob thought in class I found this kid. After batting Bob said can you make it here Saturday at 9am. He said yes Bob thought great. The next morning Bob saw Caitlin said how are you today she said fine. Caitlin said do you eat lunch in the cafeteria Bob said yes. Caitlin said lets eat together. Bob said sure we can talk a little more. When lunch came Bob sat with Caitlin, Bob said I am very busy because I am also the baseball coach building a team. Caitlin said do you need a coach, Bob said yes two of them. Well she said I can coach. Bob said we play 30 games a year 15 of them away. Caitlin said I can make the games no problem with me. Bob said you are one then. What we need is uniforms for the team we need sponsor to find. Caitlin said I will try to find one. Bob said so will I we will make a good team. Caitlin laughed said I also know who makes them. Bob said first things first sponsor first.

Giving thought to that bob got an idea went to the store where he bought the patio stuff. They said yes they would sponsor the uniforms. The next day he saw Caitlin at lunch told her he got the sponsor of the uniforms. Caitlin said great I can go to the maker and give them the order. How many she said. Bob thought and said 15 total, Two coaches and head coach are included.

Caitlin asked what color. Bob thought said shirt light blue pants darker blue should be good, with the sponsor on the back small number on the front. The cap should be lite blue with the cap darker

Caitlin said ok. Bob said find out the price I will get the money from the sponsor. They finished eating kissed both returned to their classes. Bob saw those faces again said we will get ready for a test of twenty questions. I feel since you guys were into it should be no problem. After one hour they turned in their test. Bob was right all passed their test. I told you that you were into it everyone passed.

Bob thought about his teacher saying the same thing. Well now it was the end of the week on Saturday the team practices. Bob got there 8:30am saw the team coming in on bikes cars also Caitlin also was their. Bob got all the pitchers to do laps around the field. Then throw long to stretch the arms. Then bob did infield practice while Caitlin hit to outfield. Bob also wanted hitting practice.

When it came time for hitting Bob told the pitches to throw straight no curves. Ten hits apiece then lay a bunt down. Bob saw Caitlin while hitting was going on talked about the team how it is shaping up.

I had to see what kind of team you will have. Bob asked what she thought they have promise she said.

Bob said I think so to. Caitlin said I played fast pitch softball, also some track & field too. Bob said you're an athlete. Caitlin said about five years ago. Bob said it is hard to hit fast pitch softball. Caitlin said I pitched as well. Bob said I also played baseball in N.Y. for the high school. But when I graduated college with masters degree I did not want to teach there. I traveled a lot found this town to come to teach. Caitlin said I was born here would like to see other places. I will be glad to take you to N.Y. You will see plenty a jungle of people. while talking they saw guys ripping the ball they looked like very good. It was the big right hand to pitch bob said throw no curves let them hit, you would strike them out otherwise. After the practice Bob told the right hand that he would start in the first game. After the practice Bob went home to paint the kitchen get that out of the way.

Bob turned on the tv watched a program about wild animals about 6pm the bell rung it was Caitlin Where Are we going. Caitlin said you are a history buff lets go. I will direct you then you will see.

When they got there it was a frank shaped store. Bob said ok lets go in. Caitlin said what are you Thinking. Bob said a frank store hope the foods good. Caitlin said I eat here often food is very good Bob read the menu said they have lots to offer then franks. Caitlin said you got to try their hotdog.

Bob said ok order for me what you think I washing up. Bob returned his dish was filled with a hot dog, french fries, two pickles. After eating their dish they had coffee and cake.

Bob said that was a decent meal Caitlin. They left to see a drive in movie when they got there Bob Said its years since I been to a drive in movie. Caitlin said this has been here for twenty years.

They got to their spot hooked the speaker in their window waited till the movie started. The Movie was the unforgiven with Clint East wood. Bob saw the movie in N.Y. a while back. Told Caitlin said it's a good movie. I do not mind seeing it again. What I remember about drive in Movie is the many who make out. Caitlin asked do you want to make out. Bob said yes kissed Caitlin. Both were going good when Bob said Caitlin to do this right lets wait till movie over then At the house we can continue.

When the movie ended they left to Bobs home. When they got their entered the house both were stripping their clothes Bob picked up Caitlin carried her to the bedroom

Where they continued their love making. Around 10:30 Caitlin said I got to go home. Bob said your A great girl I will see you at school. Bob stayed up till 11pm felt tired then went to his bedroom to Sleep. When Monday came Bob left for school. When he got there after parking his car he went Into the school to his room was 10 minutes before class. This gave Bob time to write on board what Text they were going to go over. The boys came into class at 9am they set down saw the board

Got ready for Bob to teach. Bob saw they were ready so he told them to go to page 12 in text. Then Said Friday I will give out a twenty question test on what we went over you should have no problem.

Bob went over the text with the class asked if any question ask me know. The class was very studious Bob felt this class is into this text should have no problem on Friday. The bell rung for lunch Bob Met Caitlin they ate lunch together. Bob asked Caitlin were are you taking me for supper. Caitlin said To another place you should like history buff. Bob said ok I can wait. When the day was at 3pm Bob Went home to wait for Caitlin. At 6 pm she came they went to this new place when they got there it was a rail wood car restaurant. Bob thought this is something else. When they entered they ordered What Caitlin said was good.

After dessert they left to Bobs home. They put on the tv sat close Sometimes kissing. When it got to 10:30pm Caitlin said I better go my godmother worries about me. Bob said there is going to be a day where you stay here. I am in love with you, Caitlin said I love you As well. After Caitlin left Bob thought I got to get her a ring. Bob turned off the tv went to bed Took a book he was reading with him.

About 1130pm Bob put book down turned off the light Went to sleep. The next day Bob after 3pm went to mall saw a popular Jeweler went in looked at Several rings un till one hit him it was what he wanted. Bob put it on a pay system for 6months. Bob took the ring in a little box thought he would give it to Caitlin at lunch then left.

Bob walked the mall saw a sports store. Went in saw a baseball counter thought he would use A counter for pitchers. He paid for it then went home. At home he knew Caitlin will not be here tonight so he got comfortable then put on tv watched a baseball game then turned off tv when The game was out of hand. Grabbed his book took it to the bedroom then read un till 11pm then Turned off lights went to sleep. The next day a special day in their life when Bob gives ring to Caitlin.

The next day came Bob put ring in his pocket In box it came with it. At school when the lunch bell Rang Bob was feeling good met with Caitlin said I have something for you, took the small box gave It to Caitlin she opened it saw a ring looked at Bob then tears came from her. Bob said why tears she Said I wanted this to happen I love you so much. Bob went to her kissed her said put on the ring.

Caitlin put the ring on when teachers nearby came over to congratulate them. Both had to go to class At 3pm the bell rang ending class. Bob stayed cleaned the room up then went home. The next day Caitlin told Bob that she got the uniforms will bring them to next practice. Bob said let me see The coaches uniforms. Caitlin went to her car with Bob to look at the uniforms. Bob said they Look good the team should like them. Took his uniform home with him.

At the field Bob got the team together said the uniforms came in I will give you yours after practice. But do not wear them till our first game in two weeks. After practice all joined at the car to take their uniforms Bob told them put them in your cars. Caitlin said Bob follow me to my home.

Bob said ok lets go. When they arrived Bob met her godmother who knew a lot about Bob. Your all she talks about. Caitlin I would like to talk to Bob alone ok she said. She told Bob that Caitlin lost her mom dad in a car crash at age 14. I took her since that tragic situation. Caitlin Showed me the ring I think that was great she loves you. Bob whenever you marry I saved up for This day to come I would like to pay for the wedding affair. Bob said that is very nice of you.

The lady called for Caitlin said he is a very nice young man. I am happy for you. Bob thought That is why she did not want me to pick her up. Then the lady went to kitchen came back with coffee Some crackers. Then said did you eat supper yet no said Caitlin, I have something I made will get It and warm it up. She said hold off on the crackers. She came out with lasagna then put out Plates to eat. Bob I have wine if you drink it. Bob said no but if you have a soda that will be great.

She got two cans of soda out then gave it to Bob and Caitlin. She poured wine for her self. After they Ate, Bob said I enjoyed that meal the lady said when will you guys marry. Bob said Caitlin pick out a Month you like then we will set it up. Caitlin said there is one more place I want you to see. Bob said Ok we will go there tomorrow.

The end of week Friday came then after the bell rings at 3pm Bob gets With Caitlin want to go there now or 6pm. Caitlin said I will see you at 6pm. Bob went home then At 6pm when Caitlin came they left to another place. When they arrived Bob saw a nice place on top of a hill with a big driveway.

It was a log cabin a big one very nice inside after eating salmon fish Followed up with coffee and pie Bob thought nice place I like it very much. Caitlin said my favorite Now my favorite Bob said. We have practice Saturday we better get home get some rest. I really Liked that place Bob said really sharp place to eat. I saw a big room I guess they have parties there. Caitlin said yes they have weddings etc. they went to Bobs home laid on the couch watched tv Kissed several times. At 10pm Caitlin said I better get home see you at practice Saturday. Bob Said ok get home safe. Caitlin said I was thinking about the month and it should be September.

Baseball will be over it would be less on you, Bob said September it is. They kissed goodnight Bob took his book to bedroom to read. The next day at the field they had practice it went very well Bob feels this team is very good. After practice Caitlin said I have to get your ring.

Bob said can I help you no she said its my duty. Caitlin went to the same jeweler picked out a ring For Bob put a down payment on a six payment plan. The next day at lunch she gave Bob his ring. Bob said very nice put it on then kissed Caitlin. Bob then said Caitlin we have to decide where This wedding will be held. Caitlin said I think here because it would be hard for people to come.

Bob said ok then said what about the log cabin room. Caitlin said that would work well. Bob said

We go there pick a date in September line things up tonight. Caitlin said I will come to your home Whenever your going there. Bob said how about Tuesday after class we can eat there. Bob said bring your aunt she will like to see the pace. Caitlin said she surely would like to come. When Tuesday came Bob at lunch told Caitlin we can go right after classes. At six we have practice. It will give us plenty of time. All went to cabin and ate supper had coffee and pie. The aunt said very nice place plus thank you or thinking of me. I enjoyed myself Bob said it is were we will have dinner.

On our wedding day. Bob said we are going to place our time now with the manager. The aunt said It will be a pretty nice place to have dinner. The aunt said how many people you figured would come. Bob said on my end my parents my sisters my be a teacher or two. Bob said not sure how many on Caitlin side. I am not sure but no more then a fifty people total. The date was set with manager then They went home. Caitlin car at Bobs house she took aunt home. The practice at 6pm still to go Bob got ready to go to field. It was now 5pm still time to go. Bob decided to try on uniform then got It out put it on. Bob liked the uniform colors it came out well.

Then Bob dressed to go to field. He was early there so he got the bats balls together then the team came as did Caitlin. Since it was practice Bob again told all pitchers to lap the field then throw long to get arms ready to throw.

Caitlin hit to outfielders they threw to different bases. Bob did infield by having them do double play Then throw to second and home. Then they got ten hits apiece then lay a bunt down run to first. After they finished hitting Bob called them together said our first game is coming soon in two weeks.

We will have four more practices then we play for real. I think this team is solid should win lot of games Bob then said remember Saturday here again we will do the same thing my be before our first game we will have two games from our team split I will let you know what side your on.

Bob then said you all can leave see you Saturday. Bob collected bats balls put in car then left.
Caitlin went home because of long day Bob agreed said he would go to bed early. The time was 8pm Bob was tired took shower then a book to bed. At 10pm put book down Turned off light then slept. At 7pm Bob got up ate then dressed for school. At 8am he left For school. Bob was in class at 845am put on the board to days page of history to share.

Bob liked his class they were very studious. Class he said remember our Friday test study. The bell rung for lunch and Bob met Caitlin shared a table ate lunch talked about first game. Caitlin told Bob that the team we are playing won last year with 22 wins. Bob said our team Will win more. After lunch back to class Bob thinking about what Caitlin said thought about Baseball team. After class he got a call from a young transfer from Philadelphia who told Bob His family moved here because of job, that he pitched for the high school team he wanted to play. Bob told him to come to the field after class at 4pm bring a glove I will see what you can offer.

Bob was thinking should be good player if pitched for team. When class ended Bob headed for Playing field met the young man who was 6ft 180 pounds athletic looking boy. Bob said to him Tell me what was your record there last year he said 7 wins 2 loses. Bob said go to mound pitch no curves just throw to me. After 20 throws Bob was seeing his number two pitcher. Bob said Come to the field Saturday we are having split team game you can pitch in that game will tell me a lot The next day at lunch Bob told Caitlin we now have our number two pitcher. He described him as A winner. Caitlin said good two games a week two great pitchers we can go undefeated.

Bob said or very close. Friday came the class was tested again with twenty questions. After class He told the two boys on team that a new boy joined team he pitched in Philadelphia for high school. I had him throw to me I also will pitch him Saturday in our game. Bob then said he is number two. With the big right hander then this guy with you all we should win some games. Bob told them as. Coach I evaluate very fast when I see talent this kid can pitch. He told the other pitcher that he is number Three right now. Bob said three is a good spot because you might be in a lot of games. I would not Hesitate to bring you in. Bob told him that this team now is headed to a close undefeated season.

We have bats defense now three good pitchers. I might even use you to close games do not feel bad. The boy said what is best for the team is ok with me. Bob said that is the spirit I want from you When Saturday came everybody was ready to play at the school grounds. Bob had the big guy pitch For one team for 4 innings the number three guy pitch 5 to 7 the other team the second pitcher For the other team for 7 innings. Bob said when the game goes on I will see who I can play.

The game started the big righthander was the home team so the game started. The pitcher From Philadelphia started through three innings no runs on either side. Bob thinking boy What a duo. Bob asked him how he was feeling said fine. Bob said two more game over. After five scoreless Bob took out the big guy. The third guy pitch the rest of the game. Bob let other guy to pitch 7 innings. The game halted in 7 with a score of 2 to 1. Bob said Great game good pitching from both sides. The Philadelphia pitcher won acclaim from team. Caitlin said to Bob you know talent when you see it. It is scary what the two will do this year. Caitlin said we will find out next week we are playing last year winner. Bob said they do not Scare me. Bob told everyone Tuesday practice we will go over fundamentals. They all went home.

Bob said to Caitlin come over at 6pm we will go to movie. The time was 12noon so plenty of time To go home shower then relax. When he got home he ate lunch watching tv news then turned off tv. Took a book to read and relaxed. Bob thought he would want a patio looked outside saw that He could put one 20x20. He took a ride to store that bought uniforms asked about patio supplies They told him about a guy who works at putting them in he took number talked to him the guy Said charge 50.00 for day. You get supplies. Bob got the cement bags with finishing tool. Got to His house unloaded it then headed to sears. Then bought outdoor furniture for patio. He called the guy Said cement in garage with finisher I will outline the 20x20 slab. The guy said I will do job on Monday.

Bob said I teach so you can just do the job everything is in garage. Bob said I get home at 3:30pm. The man said fine. When lunch bell rung Bob was anxious to tell Caitlin about patio. Caitlin said how big.

Bob said 20x20. Caitlin said sounds big. Bob said patio furniture was ordered already a man is putting it in should be done by time I get home. I have to get lights for the patio will look today. After lunch Bob went to class then the bell rung at 3pm Bob cleaned up room then went home. When home went to the back yard the man was cleaning up. Bob said good job when can I use it. The man said 24 hours It is 4 feet deep should be good to go on. Bob said can I offer you a beer. He said no water fine.

Bob got his check book wrote 50.00 gave it to the man. Handed him a bottle of water. Bob said did a nice job I will refer you if anybody needs cement work. Bob decided to go to sears for patio lights.

When the man left Bob cleaned up went to sears. Bob saw what he wanted purchased the lights. He thought right above the patio to his house. Went home installed the lights felt good about the patio.

The time was 5pm so Bob put on something to eat took it to the living room put on the tv ate while he watched the news. When the sports came on the comment of the guy was high school baseball starts next week. Will their be a winner other then last years team. Bob said yes us then smiled.

After eating decided to put on lights outside to see how it looks. Bob thought once patio furniture Comes should be nice to go on. The lights came on covered the patio nicely. Bob thought a Barbecue Friday night with Caitlin would work well. Friday came at lunch Bob told Caitlin that Friday night we stay at our house eat outside on the patio then barbecue, Caitlin said sounds great.

Caitlin then said our house. Bob said yes it is our house when we get married. Bob said I think we Will go over fundamental things in practice. Tuesday starts games our first game is away playing Last years winners. Caitlin said yes then we will see how good we are. Bob said we are real good The big guy is pitching first then Philadelphia At home our talent in pitching alone is good.

We got hitting defense a good team. The bell rung back to classes. Bob said Caitlin barbecue Tonight bring your aunt if you want. The bell rung at 3pm Bob went shopping for food items For the dinner tonight. Bob was thinking corn on cob with ribs. Also a six pack of beer.

At home by 5pm Bob started the grill outside to get it hot then put the ribs on and corn. Caitlin with her aunt came with an apple pie. Caitlin said I look for plates plus utensils. Bob said there is sauce in the fridge for ribs bring that too. Caitlin after bringing stuff out

Went back to fridge took two beers bottle of water. When finished they topped it off with coffee and pie. The aunt said real good meal I enjoyed it Bob, im glad you like it he said They talked for an hour or so Bob put on the lights. Then cleaned the grill then put on radio.

They stayed out there till 9pm. Bob said I enjoyed the patio glad I got it. I can come out here At night read a book. The aunt said I like your home good luck with it. Bob said thanks. After Caitlin her aunt left Bob cleaned up the patio and grill then found the book he wanted then Went out on patio lights still on read book on lounger he got. Bob thinking this is the life I am glad I got this patio and lounger. Bob read to 10pm felt sleepy closed book turned off patio lights.

Turned off inside lights went to bed with book un till he falls asleep. The next day Bob felt good then had something to eat then at 8:15 got ready for school. At 9am the class came in Bob had page on board.

He told class our first game is away that we were playing last year champs. Next week Tuesday we start. Bob then said what you learn I will give you Friday a twenty question test you should have no problem. A pupil yelled out who will pitch the first game Bob answered our big righthander. This is Wednesday just a few more days our team will play. We practice Saturday I will go over fundamentals once more.

I feel strongly about team winning most games we play but there always something surprising. The bell rung for lunch Bob met Caitlin they ate lunch then talked about team practice Saturday.

Bob sad this day we will go over fundamentals have that intrenched then hitting. Caitlin said we have a strong team the team we play Tuesday will test us. Bob said very strong I really see us in the hunt for the championship. Caitlin said if we win Tuesday you might be right. They went back to class then at 3pm the bell rung all went home. Bob went to the gym asked Jim if he was going to game.

Jim said yes this is last years champ we are playing. Bob said we should leave about 6pm. Jim agreed.

Thursday the principle went on the mike telling all who are interested in Tuesday baseball game to leave at 6pm. The baseball team bus has room for others first come first served. The bus holds about 100 the team takes half the bus. Bob in class anyone going to game Tuesday three hands went up. Bob said get to field about 5:30pm should get in bus. At lunch time Bob asked the Principle if she was going to game.

She said yes I will go in bus with team. Bob then said get there at 5:30 pm no problem getting seat. Bob thought good now we better win. After lunch Bob returned to class went over several pages remember class Friday test. The bell rung the class left Bob cleaned up board then left. Knowing he would not see Caitlin tonight thought to order a pizza pie then when it delivered got a soda then put on tv.

Bob found news at 4pm then waited for sports to come. They said the high school teams play Tuesday Our local team plays last years champs. Talking to some people watching the team says they are tough.

Should be a good game. Bob laughed thought how nice to be on tv news sports. After eating Bob took a book to patio to read. After two hours out there Bob felt to close lights leave patio go to bedroom. Bob did just that un till 10pm felt sleepy turned light off went to sleep. Friday came then Bob at school gave class test while waiting he looked at lineup of team for any changes. The time was moving the first test was put on his desk. Ten minutes left they all put test on desk. Bob looked at all test was not surprised That they all passed Bob told class you all passed the test will look to go over our next chapter

Monday. The bell rung class left for lunch Bob met Caitlin they walked to lunch room then sat to eat.

Bob well our practice is next then real games. Bob said we have several people going with us including the Principle to game Tuesday. I fell that this team is two strong to lose many games if any. Caitlin said win this game anything is possible. Bell rings back to class Bob asked class to go to next chapter lets begin on page 26. Bob taught class that many nations get strong then collapse but Rome was so big at this time its demise was shock to many. Leadership is crucial but what happened to Rome was poor leadership. with the burning of Rome came its demise. The bell rings again the class leaves Bob cleans board then leaves for home. Its Friday night Bob makes a cheese on toast sandwich with a soda puts on tv looks for news finds it then starts eating. Sports comes on talks about the first game we play against last year champs. They said the rummer is this local team is strong will give tough game. Bob tells the tv you bet were strong. Caitlin told Bob that she will be with aunt tonight shopping. Bob alone will get his book go out to patio read book in lounger. Time moves on and when it got to 10:30pm Bob went to bedroom to read and when he felt sleeping put book down shut off the light to sleep.

The next day practice Bob was up early 7am then ate then took off to field.
Page 21

When Bob got to field he got things ready then team showed up as did Caitlin Bob told team What I want today is go over fundamentals. Then we will hit twenty apiece. First when we walk A batter pitchers I want you to throw to first keep him close. What I want to show is we know he Is there. Second pitch outs this league steals a lot so catchers watch for this. Now lets practice this Second baseman go out to cover, first basemen go out to play first. Asked one player to go to first then try to steal. Catcher watch runner. The runner went yell steal the catcher threw to second got the runner.

That the way to throw Bob yelled. Got another runner on first another on second Bob said this very good to learn were to throw. Puts a man on third base now the count is important as are how many outs. Also who is a very fast runner. Right now we do not know many answers so if one out be on lookout for bunt.

27

If it is a double steal get the second runner at third. Lets say no bunt but they are going catcher you have to be very alert to throw to third base. If it is a hit ball to infield try double play we must get one. Bob says if you watch many major league games they work on this as well. Bob tells a hitter to get up puts himself as pitcher gets two men on to see what happens if ball hit to infielder. Bob tells them one out lets play hitter hits ball to second basemen who try double play and gets it. Bob tells him very good then throws another ball when it pops up to third basemen three out. Bob says catcher I want to put a man on first catcher watch for the steal. On the third pitch runner goes Bob yells going catcher rears up throws him out.
That is the way to throw catcher. This is what I want you infielders to think about each game we play.

Very important stuff. Bob then says play all positions we are hitting now. After they all hit Bob tells the team I think were ready for them I will say without any question you should win most games.

Bob reminds them wear your uniform Tuesday meet the bus at 5:30 pm. Have a good weekend see you Tuesday. Caitlin said that was a good stuff you showed them. Bob said were we going tonight how about staying home barbeque Bob said sounds good ok. I will pick up some things see you at 6pm.

Bob went shopping got what he needed to fill himself and Caitlin. Bob got everything going when Caitlin came at 6pm then went to patio saw Bob cooking said smells good. Bob says it is good.

Bob cooked ribs corn on cob tells Caitlin get dishes its ready. Caitlin gives Bob the dishes when he puts the ribs and corn on then gives Caitlin a dish tells her to grab two beers. Then they sat at table and ate. The radio was playing all was good. Caitlin said I got a pie we can have coffee with. Bob said sounds good. After they ate then had coffee plus pie Caitlin & Bob sat looking at tv watched tv for two hours with off and on kissing. Caitlin tells Bob she has to go feeling tired Bob kissed her said get home safe. Bob also feeling tired too a book to bed read till 10:30pm put book down turned off the lights went to sleep. The next morning ate then went to garage for the mower then mowed the backyard.

When finished he showered then relaxed a while then got idea to go to mall look around. When at the mall met ed the gym coach who said first game Tuesday. Bob said yes should be great game. Ed left saying see you Tuesday. Bob walked bought a ice cream cone continue walking saw sears went in looked around.

He saw sale on a drill then bought it thinking will need one for the house. Bob then left for home then when there put the drill in garage. Feeling to read got his book then went outside to lounger. At 5pm he put book down went to kitchen put on something to eat then put on tv to hear any news weather sports.

When the sports came on there was talk on the high school team its first game Tuesday. Bob liked what they said. After sports Bob turned off tv went to patio with book sat in lounger to read. The book was a story about leaders in history. Bob was a fan of Winston Churchill who was a painter too above all his other endeavors. Bob read for two hours now 7pm put book down went to his office to see if he could improve his lineup. Looking at lineup decided to move two players one was a great bunter moved

Him to 2nd batter. The other player to sixth spot because he could hit. Looked at the revised lineup felt good about it. Bob then turned on tv to the history channel was showing Germany Cities after war.

Bob a history buff enjoyed the show then at 9:30pm turned tv off took book to bed with him. When it got to 11pm put book down went to sleep. The next day Bob went to class was there 8:30am put on board page of next teaching. Cleaned off the desks when the class came in they said hello to Bob

Anxious about Tuesday game. Bob said no I feel secure about what we can do. Go to page on board.
Time moved when the bell for lunch rang. Bob met Caitlin told her that he felt looney without her.

Caitlin said I cannot wait too. They kissed then got lunch ate together then kissed again as they went to class. The principle went to Bobs class said already for Tuesday game. Bob said yes I revised lineup.

Feel real good about our chances. The principle said see you at the bus game day at 5:30pm. then left. Bob said everyone has interest in game. Time moves the bell rings at 3pm class leaves.

Bob wipes board down then leaves for home. At home Bob makes something to eat then goes to tv watches news to see what is going on. Bob knows he will not see Caitlin tonight because of game. they play ball Tuesday Bob feels confident his team will play well. Time passed now its Tuesday.

Bob goes to school enters class at 8:30am puts on board next chapter page. Class arrives at 9AM

Some with smiles on their face. Bob ask why the smiles they said the game is tonight. Bob says

I well aware of that. I should tell you I am confident of my chances to win. Now go to page 12

Learn about what your getting tested on this afternoon. The bell rings for lunch Bob meets Caitlin

Kisses her says are you ready for tonight. Caitlin says that I am excited is all. Bob says me too.

They ate lunch walked back to their classes Bob kissed Caitlin see you later. Bob gave test to class then when they handed it back they all passed Bob said very good you all passed. The bell rang 3pm

Bob cleaned the board as the class left they said win tonight. Bob went home got uniform out had something to eat then put on uniform went to garage for bag of balls & bats. Put everything in car. Saw it was 4pm sat in living room watched tv till 4:45 then left for field.

Bob got to field at 5pm saw that Ed had driven the bus to front of school. Bob said hi Ed good for getting bus here. Bob put items in the bus now waiting for team and people. The first to come was the principle then the ballplayers then those going to game. Bob said 5:30 ready to go. The bus filled. It took them 45 minutes to get to the high school field. Bob said ok we are here lets get off both exits are open. Bob got the balls and bats asked the ballplayers help carry them. They walked to field which the other team was practicing. Bob met the manager said good game should be. He said your team can take the field if you want. Bob had infield practice as Caitlin was hitting to outfield. The game time is 7pm now 6:15pm Bob gave hitters 5 balls each to hit then said lets Play the game. The umpires came went over rules then said home team take the field. Bob showed lineup then umpire said play ball. The first batter lined out to third base. The second batter singled the third batter lined a ball down the line we had men on first and third. The clean up hitter hit to left field our runner on third scored. When he threw to home our runner on first went to second base.

Our next batter popped up. Bob told his pitcher to give it his all their first batter hit a grounder to short. The second batter struck out the third batter popped up to first. Score after one 1to 0.

The first batter singled the second batter bunted him to second. The third batter lined a single to right scoring run. The next batter hit a ball to left field. The next hit a grounder to short. Their first batter struck out their next batter popped up to third the next batter singled to left the next struck out. the next batter popped up to third. 2 to 0 in second inning. Third inning our first batter hit grounder to short our second batter the shortstop lined one over the left field fence. He got raves from everyone.

The next batter singled then the manager came out to see his pitcher. Our next batter hit ball to left for out. 3 to 0 their first batter struck out their second batter popped up to first. Their third hit to our center fielder still 3 to 0. By the sixth inning it was 5 to 0 By 7 inning 7 to 0

When the big right hand went into the bottom of ninth he was excited breezed through for win.

Bob went to the other manager shook hand said good game. Bob went to the pitcher said good game. the principle came to Bob said great game coach. Bob told team great game lets go home now. They went to bus made sure everyone who came with them was on. They got home at 10:30 pm and all were happy with win. At home school they disbursed all people off bus Bob took balls bats to car he told team come to house Saturday after practice for barbeque. Thursday home game was with a high school not so good. After all left Bob went home put things in garage then went to take a shower. Then took a book to bed with him. When it got to 12pm Bob went to sleep. The next day came Bob got up and made something to eat then went to school. When the class came in they saw the score on the board said to Bob great win. The principle went on the mike said our baseball team won 7 to 0 over last years champ. Come see them for our home game. Bob tells class that they should go to page 15 in book continue our look at demise of Rome. The bell rings for lunch Bob meets Caitlin kisses her then they ate lunch. Bob tells Caitlin sending the man on third to home was good move it moved our man to second. Thank you said Caitlin it looked good to me. Bob tells Caitlin that he promised a barbeque to team on Saturday after practice. I should invite Ed. Also.

Kisses Caitlin then goes to gym tells Ed of barbeque then goes to class. Continues the education on Rome then tells class remember test on Friday. The bell rings class leaves Bob cleans board then leaves for home. At home Caitlin car in driveway Bob walks in house Caitlin said that she misses him they kissed went to bedroom made love Bob said not to far away from living here. Caitlin said wished it were here already. They kissed Bob asked if she wants to have supper with him. Let me call my aunt first. Caitlin called aunt told her of staying to have supper with Bob. That she will be home not late. They got steaks out of fridge then put them on the grill outside with corn cob.

They ate then had coffee some crackers. Caitlin said that was good. Bob said we do it again Saturday

Barbeque for team after practice. Bob turned on tv Caitlin embraced in his arms watching movie when it ended at 8pm Caitlin said I better go home my aunt is waiting on me. Bob said ok love see you Tuesday at lunch. Bob turned on history channel saw they were showing digging for things.

Decided not for him changed channel to baseball between Yanks and Baltimore it was in seventh Baltimore leading 5 T0 3. Bob decided to watch the ending. Which Baltimore won 7 to 4. At home.

Bob then got his book to read in bed. At 11:30 put book down turned off lights went to sleep. Next Day Bob got up made some thing to eat then left to school. Bob asked how many in here going to game tonight. Twenty hands went up he knew the field seats limited to 300. Bob asked Ed what thought. Ed said we have chairs in gym. Bob asked how many Ed said 50 Bob said we may need all of them. Ed said twenty five on each end. So the day went the time was near Bob went home put on uniform at 5pm had something to eat then left to field. Ed was there lets get chairs. Took bus to gym put the chairs in bus back to field put twenty five on each side of stands. Now 6pm Bob saw stands filling up people going for chairs. We should have a crowd tonight. The umpires came went over rules at 6:30pm said home team hit the field Caitlin third base coach Ed first base coach.

Bob tells team just play good before our school. Bob told pitcher to warm up earlier he was ready. the first batter struck out the second batter ground ball to short third batter popped up to catcher.

Our first batter singled to left our second batter bunted him to second third batter singled to score our shortstop drove the ball past the center fielder wound up on third base. Next batter drove ball to right field scoring runner. Next batter hit grounder to second base score 2 to 0 our pitcher was in good form breezing through 5 innings the score 7 to 0. By ninth score was 12 to 0. Game over.

Two games other teams did not score. After game principle said she would order more stands.

Bob and Ed returned the chairs to the gym shook hands of win then went home. Bob showered took uniform to washing machine put some powder I n the machine washed the uniform. Bob then Had a sandwich to eat while watching tv news when sports came on commented on school two wins How good they looked how nice the uniform was. Now if they keep winning they could be champs This year. Their next game is going to be tough because they have some good hitters placed second.

Last year. The next day at school a banner was put up go champs. Bob said the interest was high. That he was glad to see the interest. Bob went to class got high fives from class. He told class that they should go to page 20 to continue the education. After a while the bell rings for lunch. Bob meets Caitlin kisses her then got there lunch ate together talked about next game which was away. After lunch they went to classes. Bob had the interest of class explaining chapter they talked about. The Bell rings at 3pm class leaves Bob cleans board then leaves for home. At home showers then makes supper takes it to tv area then watches news then sports. Bob then shuts tv off gets book goes to patio.

Stays out there till 10:30 comes in goes to bed at 11:30 then sleeps. The next day he is up at 7am makes something to eat then decides what he will do in practice Saturday. Tuesday game is next.

He heard they have good hitters but with the big right hand pitcher going did not fear that. The day was Friday and the day went fast when Bob got home he ordered a pizza. When it came he took it to tv area watched news then sports then history channel. Today the history channel had a look at divers searching for treasure from sunk ships. When it ended Bob was still eating pizza. The time was now 6pm Bob shut off tv went to patio with his book. When the time reached 10pm Bob came in went to bedroom with his book un till 11pm then turned off light went to sleep. The morning came

Bob went to garage for the bats and balls. Put them in his car then had something to eat. Time was 8am Bob left for the field. When he got there some were there already to his surprise.

Caitlin drove up then most of the team. Bob told them normal practice infield outfield 10 hits apiece.

Bob took infield Caitlin took outfield. The hitting was good to watch because the guys were hitting the ball well. After practice he said Tuesday away game should be good game. Then said see you at the field Tuesday at 5:30pm. Caitlin asked Bob we doing anything tonight. Bob said yes eat out movie pick one you want to see. Bob went home as did Caitlin it was 1pm Bob mowed the yard then took it easy watched movie then saw ball game he watched for awhile then turned off tv had a nap.

At 5pm he went showered dressed then turned on tv news. 6pm Caitlin came they left to go to dinner movie. After they came back to Bobs home made love then at 10pm Caitlin went home. The next day Sunday. Bob saw that his Yankees were playing at 1 pm at Red Sox. He planned to watch game. When it got close to game time Bob made lunch got to tv area put game on while eating lunch after eating stayed as game was tied in 7inning when Jeter hit home run to right. The game ended 1to 0 Yankees won.

Bob thought how much pitching can be in any game. The game took 4 hours.

Bob decided to get his book go out on patio to read awhile. Bob stayed on patio till 7pm. Then went in to make supper. He had several dinners to choose from took one put in microwave waited half hour when he took it out then put on plate took to tv room watched news. After he switched to travel channel they were showing Switzerland with its attributes. It was for hour had Bob intrigued.

Then he switched to anything that interest him. There was a channel called pawn shop that held

Bob interest as people brought in strange items. When it got to 9pm Bob had enough shut off tv went to bedroom with his book read till 10:30 put book down turned off light went to sleep. The morning came Bob was up at 7am then ate then headed to school. At school headed to his classroom.

Was told he has a hard game Tuesday. The team they were playing was in third place last year now with new ball players added won their first two games. Bob went on to teach not discuss baseball.
Page 29 when the bell rang for lunch Bob met Caitlin they sat together ate lunch. Bob asked what do you know of team we play Tuesday. She said they won close games against poor teams. Bob said the class said it will be tough game. Caitlin said we are better then they are plus big right hand goes against them. Bob tells Caitlin I love you then kisses her. The bell rings they go back to classes. When the bell rings at 3pm class leaves one guy said I saw your

team play you should beat them. Bob felt good then went home. The time was April 4th Monday Bob went to garage got mower then mowed the front yard. Then Bob put on something to eat turned on tv news. When the sports came on they talked about the battle coming up between our team theirs. Bob thought my team very good should win. Bob went over lineup saw no flaws then got his book went to bed reading till 10:30 then slept.

Tuesday came off to class Bob went. When class came in Bob said I reviewed game tonight my thought is the other team will get its first lost. The class was then told to go to page 45 lets learn.

With smiles on their faces Bob asked why the smiles they said the other team beat lower schools your team beat the best. Bob said that is why I said we will win. Bob then said we will see tonight.

Bell rings for lunch Bob meets Caitlin kisses her then they sat to eat. Bob asked ready for game she said yes. The bell rings so they go to their classes. Bob ask the class who is going tonight game.
Three hands went up be at field at 5:30pm. To go on bus. When the bell rings at 3pm Bob went home took out his uniform then cleaned up then ate then dressed for game. Watched news at 4pm weather seemed ok should be no problem away. When time got to 4:45pm Bob left for field after putting bats and balls in trunk of car. When the bus was filling up between team then pupils they left for away game that took 40 minutes to reach. Parked the bus where they saw the field then went to their positions Bob had

infield outfield hitting five balls. The umpires came went over ground rules.

Bob shook hands with other manager then his team took field. Our first batter singled to left. the second batter walked the shortstop lined a hit to center run scored now first and third 4th batter bunted up the third base line runner scored from third the third basemen made good play throwing to first for first out. Next batter hit fly ball to center caught two out. Next batter singled to left then stole second base. Next batter lined out to third. Their first batter popped up to short 2nd batter struck out next batter hit grounder to short. Our first batter singled to center next batter bunted him to second the top of lineup batter singled to left run scored now 3 to 0. The runner on first was fast stole second.

Our second batter hit the fence in left field almost home run. Scored runner batter on second third batter hit home run over fence in left. Shortstop has a big night. 4th batter lines a single to center. Our 5 batter hits single to right now first and third. The coach went to the mound replaced pitcher with another guy who threw curve balls. Our sixth batter bunts up to first base runner on third scores. They get runner at first. Score now 6 to 0. The time this game ended the final score was 10 to 1. Bob said to the team great game. Said to pitcher great game how do you feel. He said fine I had no problem at all. Bob felt good thinks his team has a chance to come in top. Bob said to the shortstop nice hitting your something else. Principle came to Bob said great game our team is very good. Bob said your right.

On the way home they all were singing take me out to the ball game. They play a high school Thursday

At home that is two wins one loss. When they got to the field Bob said great game see you Thursday

They said no practice Wednesday. Bob said no you earned a day off. He then looked for Caitlin

Told her that no practice wed, that they can meet have barbeque talk awhile. They then left to go home. Bob felt hungry put something in microwave took a beer put on tv till supper done. He heard microwave ended went took out meal looked for glove got it then took meal out to tv area put on table then ate. When finished he put on a cup of coffee had with it some crackers. The time now 10pm.

Watched tv till finished with coffee, then shut tv off then took his book to bed with him.

Bob found himself needing sleep time was 10:30pm put book down turned off lights went to sleep.

Next day Bob up early 6:30am had something to eat then got dressed for school. Left for school at 7:45 was in class 8:15 am decided to look at what he could teach today knowing that the last page he taught was page 46. When the class came in at 9am the board showed page 50 to start. They continued the course with Bob putting extra effort to make class truly understand what Rome did. the bell rung for lunch Bob met Caitlin kissed her then they got lunch then ate. Bob said come over supper tonight bring your aunt if you want. At 3pm Bob cleaned up classroom then went home but first stopped at store for some things he needed. Went home got the grill ready the table as well then started to cook the ribs. The beans & corn. At 6pm Caitlin with her aunt came then went directly to yard.

Said hi to Bob who said hi come in sit down it is ready to be eaten. They sat at table already ready with utensils, napkins. Plates etc. Bob placed racks of ribs on their plates put corn beans on big plates sat down with cooler nearby told them soda or wine in there. The radio was on low with slow music.

All all very nice setup said the aunt. Bob said thank you then they ate. Delicious said Caitlin.

Bob said yes it is. The aunt wanted wine Caitlin had soda as did Bob. Bob put on coffee then he had pound cake to serve. After that they just sat out there with the music. The aunt said thank you for a a nice supper. Bob said there will be many more to come. It was now 8pm when Caitlin said we better go big day Thursday. Upon leaving the aunt said thank you Bob for a nice time tonight. They all kissed good night. Bob cleaned the grill then cleaned up everything. Shut off radio went to tv room watched tv till 10pm shut it off took book to bed with him. Read book to 11pm felt sleepy put book down shut off light went to sleep. Next day came Bob up at 7am showered then dressed ate the left for school at 8am.

Today game day at home the school they play has 1 win two loses. With the Philadelphia pitcher slated to pitch. Bob thought to use the third pitcher 4 innings to see what he can do. At lunch time he spoke with him told him it is the best time to see what we got. Told starting pitcher what he has in mind the pitcher did not mind he understood what the coach was doing. The coach said you will be there if He fails in the first inning. Bob was glad he understood what he was trying to do was a team player.

At school lunch he told Caitlin as well. The principle saw Bob in hallway told him the new stands will help the crowd no more chairs to get. Bob said that was a pain to get rid of. In class he asked how many coming to the game later. Seventy five percent of class will be in stands. Bob then said get your book go to page 58. After this I will test you on what we gone through. When the bell rung the class left Bob cleaned board took test he gave home with him. Bob at home had something to eat got uniform on watched the news when it got to 5pm left to field with bats and balls. At the field he saw the stands starting to fill. The team came the coach had infield outfield practice no hitting as the other team came he told third pitcher to warm up that he was going to start. He was happy about that then threw a little.

To get ready. He was slated as number two before the boy from Philadelphia came won the job. The umpires came went over ground rules said play ball. Bob team took field threw ball around when their First batter came up. He hit grounder to short 2nd batter hit grounder to third 3rd batter struck out on a Nice curve ball. Our first batter singled to center our 2nd batter popped up. Our third batter lined a ball Down third base line with our runner rounding first went to third batter to second a double boy he is hot. Fourth batter lined single to right two runners scored 2 to

0. 5th batter lined to short two outs the Sixth batter singled to center runner went to third.

With runners on first and third the 8th batter bunted down third with runner scoring from third safe at first. 9 th batter popped up. 3 to 0 their first batter Struck out on curve ball the 2nd batter popped out to third. 3rd batter singled to left 4th batter popped up.

To catcher. Our first batter singled to left our 2nd batter hit a slow grounder to second which 2nd basemen threw out at first, runner on 2nd base. Third batter shortstop singled to center scoring run. 4 to0.

The pitcher for us threw four scoreless innings. Bob had him throw I more inning this game was out Of hand by sixth inning was 6 to 0. Our number two pitcher came in the sixth closed out game final Was 8 to 0. Bob congratulated him then said to team great game to shortstop you're a great hitter.

The principle came to Bob said you have put together a good team nice win. Bob said thank you. Bob got things balls bats put in car. By now everyone was gone except a few who were on team. They said good game coach Bob said get home safe. Bob left for home at home he took balls bats Put them in garage. Bob then went took shower then went to kitchen to make something to eat.

Turned on tv news then ate while watching news. When the sports came on they mentioned the Win by high school plus the home run by the third basemen. They talked about a chance to win. Bob thought yes we have a chance to win it all. Their record close to end of season was 26 wins 0 loss With 4 more games the possibility is there to go undefeated. There next game is Tuesday When Tuesday came the home game against last years winner. All week the chant was to beat them.

ThePrinciple also excited came to Bobs class said to Bob I am so excited about the team potential. Bob Said me to she laughed. Bob continued his class teaching when bell rung for lunch. Caitlin met Bob They sat together talked about the interest in team said it is getting close two more months. Caitlin Said yes I love you Bob said I love you as well. They kissed then went to their classes. When class ended. Bob cleaned room up then went home. He then had something made to eat while he was Dressing for game. After eating he put on tv news the sports part talked about game tonight Bob Thought we beat them once we can again. At the field was jammed with people the stands filled People standing behind the cage. Bob thought there into it got team together said we beat them Before have fun tonight with your school behind you.

We have a better team show them tonight. Team said yes then went to field for infield practice The other team took field for their infield then The umpires came went over ground rules then said play ball. We took to field as home team their first batter struck out 2nd batter popped up to first 3rd batter hit grounder to second base.

Our first batter singled to center 2nd batter bunted up first base line runner went to 2nd base I out. 3rd batter shortstop lined single to left runner scored from second. 4th batter doubled down the left field line runners on second and third. 5th batter hit a fly ball to center scoring man on third. Man on second Went to third base. Two outs 6 batter lined out to left field. Score now 2 to 0 they get up their first Batter hit ground ball to short one out. 2nd batter singles to left 3rd batter hits to short line drive 2 out 4th batter strikes out. By the fifth inning the score was 5 to nothing. By the 9 inning score was 5 to 0.

When they were up their first batter hits grounder to short I out. Their second batter singles to right 3rd batter lines one over the left field fence 5 to 2. Bob goes to mound sees the big guy is tired then Takes him out then gives the third pitcher the ball. Bob tells him give them your good curve ball.

After warm up he pitches he starts throwing strikes out next batter then with two out he popped up To third base. We win 5 to 2. The people go crazy principle comes to Bob I was scared when you took Our best pitcher out Bob said he was tired the pitcher I put in was capable. He proved it did he not. he principle said yes he did. Bob said three to go to himself. Told team great game good win.

The other team played well but your better. Take this great win home tonight know that you're the Best team in this league. They put their hands together thanked the lord. Bob went home put things in garage then Caitlin came in Bob sees her kisses her great win yes she said. They kiss again Bob tells Caitlin lets shower together when in shower make love after they both get dressed Bob puts on Tea had some pound cake they sit with tv on eating kissing.
When it got to 10pm Caitlin says she got to go Bob tells her get home safe love. Caitlin leaves Bob thinks of calling

parents tells them about getting married tells them stay here for awhile till I get back from honeymoon in New York. Parents told him that they can stay at there house plan for two weeks September first Saturday wedding.

Bob tells them he will show Caitlin his finance the town will go all over the place that she never went out of Iowa was 14 when she lost parents in head on crash. You will like her. Tells parents that took head baseball coaching job for extra money has team at 28 to 0 just beat last years winners today.

They said excellent job. Bob said will be good to see you guys again tell sister I love her too. Bring her too if she can come. When they hung up Bob was tired took a book to bed with him. The next day at school the principle went on mike told school about the big win. Bob smiled class clapped as Bob was putting something on board page 48 to 53 for review. When the bell rung for lunch Bob met Caitlin they kissed sat together then ate. Bob told her three games to go it is exciting to watch our team win.

Caitlin said the teams left should not be a problem. Bob said my be we can throw some innings to others. they all can play we then can see what we have to go into playoffs. Caitlin said good idea to know at least.

The bell rings for classes they kissed went to their class. Bob said to class your baseball team should go undefeated this year there is not a team left who can beat us. Bob then said with three left I can use others that can play to see what we got to go into playoffs. Bob then said go to page 60 in book lets go over it.

After about an hour talked about why did the Romans fall. Bob said I gong to test you now on that subject he gave the class a small 10 question test. They put the result on his desk Bob said continue reading pages 61 to 65 while I see what the test did. After he went over the tet he said you are a very studious class then said you all got 100. I am very proud to be your teacher. Time went on the bell rings class left Bob cleaned up then left. At home he got into very casual clothes then went into kitchen for a beer took it to living room put on tv news. When the sports came on they talked about the team that they are undefeated. That they should go all the way. The three teams left are not their caliber. Bob smiled then changed channel to pawn shop where people come in with the strangest things. Bob was going over team To see where he could make changes. To give the regulars a rest. Pitching was one left field another 2nd baseman another. Bob made lineup for Thursday game away. Had his answers put together was glad that When Thursday came he told Caitlin what lineup would be.

Caitlin said it should work well. Bell rings back to class they go. Bob speaks to them about review on Friday because we ended the Roman work I will let you know Monday about the next study bell rings class leaves as Bob cleans board.

. Bob then goes home to get ready for to nights game. First thing have something to eat then dress for game. After eating Bob got his uniform out put it on then gets the bats & balls to car.

Bob uses 25 balls 14 bats. Per game. The time was 4:30pm Bob thought to leave for field. When he got there the principle was there, Caitlin was there some team guys ready to go.

Bob said hello then put balls bats in bus. They all went on bus then sat till everyone comes. The bus Filled by 5;30pm they left for school that was 25 miles away. When they got there they went to field.

Bob had the boys help him with bats then they all went to their dugout. Bob then said tonight I am playing some other guys showed who they were said I want to see them play to see what we got. He then posted lineup on dugout wall. The umpires came Bob had infield practice then called everyone to bench he was not sure if the other team was to practice. The umpires call both managers to them went over ground rules then said play ball. We were up first when our first batter singled to left. 2nd batter lined single to right shortstop up with men on first and third lines a single to left scoring one run. 4th batter hits single to left run scores 5th batter pops out to catcher 6th batter flies deep to center caught Two out 7th batter New face singles to left. Run scores. 3 to 0 8th batter new face hits hard line out to short. Big one was pitching their first batter pops up to third 2nd batter strikes out 3rd batter grounder to pitcher he throws to first 3 outs. Our 9th batter pitcher hits grounder to short I out 2nd batter ingles to right 3rd batter lines out to third 2 outs shortstop hits home run way over left field fence. 5 to 0 final 9 to 0 after game Bob said to replacements good playing it showed me what you can do. Bob then said we got quite a team with two to go I am proud of you. Bob said to shortstop nice hit you are special. To pitcher nice game. Bob then said we can go against anybody our level. The playoffs will test that. Two to go home game then away game. Lets get on bus. The other manager said you have quite a team Bob said thank you. Got the team on bus with everyone ready they went home. The time of year was August the baseball is coming to the end. The home game was next which they won 12 to 2. The away game last of year they won 15 to 2. They will now play the district game Saturday away game. The principle got a huge trophy winning the high school baseball games. Bob saw it said to principle It is a big one. The Principle said your first year here as coach did it. My first year as principle it is just amazing. Bob said now district next. A new banner was made that said district next. The game was to be played at a college field 50 miles away. Bob had a Friday practice just to keep team in shape. Infield, outfield, hitting 10 ea.

The game was at 1pm so the team left at 10am. The bus was filled plus many cars was coming. When they got there the field was big the stands were plenty holds 10,000. The other manager was having practice

Bob saw team said no bigger then us to himself, shook hand of other mgr. We will be off you can practice in five minutes. Bob had infield then gave 5 hits each. His team was poised to give its all. After Bob said to team there not bigger then us they did not go undefeated like us we should win this why not.

They closed together lets win this they said. The umpires came 4 of them went over ground rules then Said lets play ball. We had them toss a coin for home team we won so we went out on field. It was nice Field to play on. High pitchers mound great for our big righthander. Their first batter popped to first. 2nd batter struck out 3rd batter grounder to short. The first batter for us singled to right 2nd batter bunt.

To third playing back he was safe at first the shortstop up lines double down first base line scoring two. It went all the way to back wall. 4 batter singles to right scoring man on second. Coach comes out to pitcher talks leaves him in. The score 3 to 0 5th batter hits grounder to second one out. 6th batter hits ball to right fielder two outs 7th batter singles to left 8th batter pops up to catcher. 3 outs Bob tells team good job there first batter strikes out, 2nd batter bunts to third who throws him out. 3rdbatter singles to left then 4th batter hits ball to right field caught 3 outs. The game by fifth inning was 5 to 0 then by the 7th 7 to nothing.

It was the ninth inning the big tired Bob went out called on the 2nd pitcher to close game. which he did by striking out the first batter, 2nd batter pops up to third 3rdbatter grounder to short. We win district game the team exploded on field the principle tells Bob great game the other mgr. Said great job.

Bob shook his hand said good game. The other manager said you had the pitching Bob said first thing I put together. They had the district winner in the middle of field took pitchers gave them trophy which Bob handed to principle. It was huge trophy which the principal stated another huge trophy to place.

Bob said yes in our trophy case. Everyone with the school got on bus then it left to go home. The news at 6pm told the radio listeners that the school won district. Bob and Caitlin went to eat supper when they were stopped by admires. Bob gave his signature signed many peoples hats etc. Caitlin the same thing

After they got away they went to eat at the frank house then went to Bobs home made love. Their wedding coming up soon in September. It was now 18 of August Bob class got new teaching rules. It was Monday

Bob had new thing to teach about Viet Nam as he was amused at the subject matter. Bob told class that this subject matter would hit them hard. Aa lot of people died in this place. Bob said to go to page 75 which will go over the subject matter. After going over subject matter Bob told class to study pages 80 to 85 we will explore that tomorrow the bell rung for lunch. Bob met Caitlin kissed her then sat with her for lunch. Caitlin asked Bob now that baseball is over what will you do. Bob responded to her by saying marry you is next. Caitlin said you have not said what you would do. Bob said have no plans.

Bell rings so they went to their classes after kissing. Bob asked class to go over pages 80 to 85 so that your very comfortable with it. This afternoon I will talk on to you on this matter. At 3pm the bell rings

Class left as Bob cleaned off board. Bob thought that subject will be a little harder to understand as the Things that made this a bad war. Bob went home showered then got casual then put in microwave a Dinner took out a beer put on tv news sports. When the sports came on they talked about the school Winning the district plus having undefeated season. Mentioned Bob the pitching the shortstop. Said if Their together next year should repeat with their talent. Bob said yes to that remark when it ended Bob Turned off tv then took his book out to patio sat in lounge read till 10:30 pm then went to bed. The next Day he was up at 7am ate then headed to class when he parked he saw a big car in front never saw before He went in the principle saw him told him to come to her office. When he entered office a big man said My name is David Yokes I manage Iowa College baseball team for the last twenty years. I saw what you did this year. I am going to retire and need a good coach to take my place. If you are interested Come out to the college speak to me about everything. Bob looked at the principle said thank you For the opportunity I will think on it. They shook hands and he left. The principle said Bob everyone Will want you to coach you in this case should see what it offers you. He thanked her then went to class Bob asked class how many seniors are here twenty hands went up Bob asked them were they will go They said different things. But four said Iowa college. He then told the class his offer from the coach. They said yes we will have you as our history teacher. Bob said I have not agreed to it yet I have to goTo college meet the coach find out things first. Bob then said ok lets do some work on pages 80 to 85.

The time went the bell rings at 3pm. Bob seeks out Caitlin tells her what happened she said if you get That job it will be more money for sure. Bob said I did not say yes or no I have to go meet him in his Office learn what it offers. I will do that after school Thursday. Caitlin said I went to that school. It is a big school. Bob asked how many miles from our house. Caitlin said not far only 10 miles Bob then said close to home too. Well when I speak to coach I will know. Bob said I will see you Take care. Caitlin said I am excited for you. They both left, Bob decided to go to library.

He picked up a book on Iowa college. Then went home got casual ate supper then took book out to Patio started to learn about the college. What he learned was it was old respected place with a good ports program including a football team. There was not a negative thing he could find other then does He want to leave high school. He put book down went to tv put it on looked at baseball playoffs. His Mind was on seeing the coach. The time went it was 10:30 pm Bob turned off tv went to bed. The next Day came Bob up at 7am showered dressed then ate something then went to school. Bob went to class Put on board what he would talk about. The class came in at 9am sat down when Bob said go to page 84 Where it talks about what got it started. Bob said this war was not popular just recently they put a stone Slab of who died in war. It was just recently that they gave that to those soldiers. He went on to speak Of a friend of his who lived but had a very dangerous job as tunnel rat. Telling class that Viet Con army Had many tunnels.

The area was a jungle with tigers etc. a terrible war. With U.S. power they were in Constraint as to how much they can do. Bob said I want you to study all you can test Friday 10 questions The bell rings for lunch. Bob meets Caitlin kisses her they eat lunch talk about him meeting coach. Bob Said that when I do meet the coach a lot will be on what I earn there. Bell rings they go back to class. They continue the talk on Viet Con and its aftermath. The time goes bell rings for 3pm class leaves as Did Bob as he headed to the college. When he got there the office took him to coaches office when he Saw Bob he shook his hand told him sit down any questions. Bob asked him I teach history how does that work. The coach said you will teach history here in this school. The coach then said compared to What you received at your school we pay 46,000. Bob what about coaching he said 18,000 year.

Bob said that is 64,000 a year. I make now coaching 5,000 teaching 27,000 32,000 year.

When can I start here Bob said in two weeks the coach said. Bob said no way I turn this down I have a wife next month baby to follow need to make the money to handle that. This way she does Not have to work. The coach said I will want to stay see my son play. What position does he play

Bob asked The coach said catcher. I will stay for the first 10 games then retire to Florida. By the way Bob this will be your office. Bob said for the first 10 games I would like to have you as third base coach. Then tell me about who we play what you think of each team. The coach said sure I will do that for you. Coach I have a great player on my team that I think will earn scholarship to any college he wants to play.

The coach said if he is that good get him here. Bob said this was a great meeting you got me coach I ill bring what you brought here a great baseball career take team to the top. Coach said I am glad you Are replacing me because what you did in your first year was amazing at a new school. Bob said I take Anything I do very serious. I will talk to that player see what he has in mind. They shook hands again

Bob left looking the school over thinking wait till I talk to Caitlin. Got home at 6pm went to kitchen Took out a dinner from freezer put in microwave took also a beer went to tv put it on looked for news When dinner finished he got a hand towel took it to tv room ate while watching tv news. After he ate He called Caitlin told her he took job at college starts in two weeks. The money was the reason it was Hard to believe 64,000 total wow Caitlin said. Bob then said when a child comes to us you do not have to work. That is great news Bob yes it is said Bob. I start in two weeks he tells Caitlin. Bob says I have to tell the principle next time I am in school. At home Bob gets beer out goes to patio then sits In lounger with book on college he is going too.

Pleased with going to college to teach, coach 2 weeks. Time moves to 10pm Bob puts book down goes to bedroom continues to read till 11pm then goes to bed. The next day up at 7am showers gets dressed eats then leaves for school. At school he heads for principle Walks in to her room says I have important news for you. Bob says get another history teacher As I have taken the job at Iowa college. Bob then tells principle his salary teaching also coaching It was so much bigger then I thought.

The principle said can you tell me who I should give your job to have no clue on teacher but coaching I can my coach can handle job because she coached the outfield for me. She also knows the team plus my way of coaching. The principle tells Bob that he will be missed.

You did what is almost impossible to do in first year. Bob I wish you well. Bob tells her two more weeks Here then to college to teach. The middle of first week Bob was giving a test from pages 90 when a lady Comes to class tells Bob said can I help you. The lady said I am your replacement they told me to teach History class today put yourself on paid vacation. Bob tell her he is on page 90 the Viet Con area. I give On Friday I give a 10 question test on page 90. Bob then said but this your class now do what you want.

Bob went to principle office tells her thank you I will always keep this school in my heart. The principle Went to Bob kissed him on the cheek. Bob told her enjoy those trophies we won do take care. Bob went Searching for shortstop found him in the gym. Talked to him about playing for him at Iowa College next Year. I am in a position to offer you a scholarship to the college for baseball. Justin said yes I would love To play for you. Bob said good I will send to your home the paperwork. Bob was glad that was over.

Now to find my number one pitcher. He also was a senior will get offers so Bob looked for him found Him in math class. Gave him the same deal at Iowa He was elated that Bob would be his coach teacher. Bob went home it was 2pm he wanted to look over the college went got a tour from personal. When they Went to the coaches office he saw Bob tells the other person I will take it from here. Sit down Bob what Were you doing just surveying the school. Bob tells coach the two best players will play for me here.

The coach said great your building a team. We had five leave Bob tells coach were they the best players.

The coach said no but team. the team is not better off coach says that two helped last year. Bob said I will look at what the team has and build on it. The coach said let me make a copy of our schedule so you can see where we play. The coach gives Bob a copy of schedule which Bob puts in His pocket. The coach said are you ready to take over the team also history class. Bob says yes I got Paid time off for two weeks. The coach said they were nice to you. Bob said I really liked the school.

But your college is much better financially. The coach said go to personal dept. get your schedule of our history class. On your days off you can read what they teach. The coach then said our school is Co-ed forty per class. Bob said that is different then my school. Bob then said I will go to get what I am scheduled to teach. When in the personal dept Bob told them he is history teacher can I get copy Of what I am teaching the class in two weeks. They printed out for Bob a copy of history class teaching. The lady said good luck with this class. Bob said I have a master degree in history should be no problem. Bob left the school was anxious to look at what they wanted to be taught. He arrived home got something to eat then relaxed on his couch with soft music playing read the history they wanted him to Teach. Bob found it different then high school but nothing he could not do. Most of what he read was Relationships with Israel, Briton, how far back they go. How we helped Briton in second world war.

Our relationship with Russia, China, Japan. Bob read on said to himself no problem at all. When it Got to 4pm Caitlin stopped by do anything today she asked. Bob said yes I went to the college met coach To personal dept. got copies of what I would be teaching. I was just reading about that. Can you handle 20 boys 20 girls in class. Bob said I can handle most anything. Unlike the High School here I am getting a team to build on. By the way the high school team will lose the shortstop, the big righthander To the college team next year.

I also mentioned you as coach to the principle. How do you feel about coaching the team. Caitlin said I would like to try it. Bob said you are the coach tell the principle. Bob then said I am going home to study up on what they gave me to teach. Bob went home got a beer then went out to patio sat in lounger to read. Bob after two hours saw enough to feel comfortable teaching what they gave him. Still almost two weeks till class. Bob went to the library to bring books back also toTake more books out.

This time they were on what he would teach. He had to beef up on dates things took place. Bob then went to the mall went to the sports store. Bob while there looked to get another counter as he would give other one to Caitlin. Bob then walked the mall looking around had lunch there then left for home. When he got home he put the counter on the table. He then decided to mow the yard after he took a book went to patio lounger to read. At 5pm put book down went inside took dinner out of freezer put in microwave. Took out a beer waited for dinner then went to tv room to watched news sports.

Bob sort of felt he needed people to talk too. Bob called Caitlin said this is no fun without you. Caitlin said I will come over at 7pm for a while. Bob watched a western when the bell rung said come in it was Caitlin.

They hug each other when Bob picked her up took her to bedroom where they made love. Bob said I cannot wait till you're here permanently. When it got to 9pm Caitlin I got to go I am not on vacation like you. Bob said it is getting close 8 more weeks. Caitlin left throwing Bob a kiss. Bob then turned off tv went to bed with book to read. The next day up at 8am he had something to eat then went to school met the principle said vacation is good when you can share it with someone. The principle said nice of you to come here. Bob said you were always great putting up stands etc. the principle said come with me to show Bob the trophies the principle said you did this for the school in your first year. Bob said my team did it I just coached. The principle said without you, would not have these trophies. Bob said I did build the team the principle said yes you did. You did something that everyone says would be impossible. Bob said I guess being so busy

Then nothing is boring. The principle said your going to great things for the college too. Bob said thank you. Bob went home feeling much better after speaking with the principle. He felt tired went out to patio laid On lounger for a nap. When it got to 5pm Bob got up went to kitchen took dinner out of freezer then put it Microwave went to tv put on the news sports.

When the dinner was cooked he took it out to the tv room Eating while watching the news. When the sports came on they spoke about the coach of high school going o Iowa College taking the managers job of baseball. The offer had to be great for him to change schools.

From what we understand the former coach is retiring, had an interview with coach whatever was said he Is going to Iowa college to be coach teacher. So he will take over as baseball coach who will take high school coaching job. He did amazing job there will sorely be missed. Bob hearing all this thought how do They get the information so fast. Bob still on week vacation went to the patio with book laid in lounger to Read. When it got to 9pm Bob rested then came into kitchen made coffee took coffee to tv room.

Watched 10pm news sports. When it was over Bob changed channel to pawn shop watched till over it was Amazing to Bob that people came in to pawn shop with a variety of unuseable items like coin sets, old Bikes, etc. Bob watched drinking coffee the rest of show. When it was 10pm Bob turned off tv then Went to bed with his book. When it went to 11:30 pm he turned off lights went to sleep. The next day Bob up at 8am had something to eat then read paper that gets sent to him every day. In the sports section There was a trade between Yanks and Cleveland Indians got catcher gave two players To N.Y. double a ball. Bob thought fair trade. Bob then cleaned up kitchen, bathrooms, then Went to garage looked around then fixed it the way he wanted. Time was 11:30am Bob Phone called is parents to say hello.

They were excited for him then he told them he got a job at Iowa College To coach baseball also teach history. My salary jumped to 64,000. Reason I took it. Caitlin now does Not have to work when a baby comes to us. I start at the college next week. I am on vacation till then. His parents said wonderful. Bob asked are you guys flying or driving here. They said flying. Bob said you can use my car when here. It will be a nice getaway for you. Call me from airport I will Pick you up. Bob felt good talking to his parents should be good for them to see our home. Bob asked s Brenda coming. They said she would not miss it yes she is coming. Bob said great I cannot wait.

When they both hung up Bob felt hungry made a sand which also got a beer took it to tv room then Watched a western that he had not seen before it was an old one that he enjoyed. Bob thought about Talking to his parents got excited about seeing them in four weeks. After the western he looked to see If any games were on found that only spots on was golf so he looked at that for awhile when he got tired Then turned off the tv. Bob thought only four more weeks till I get married my be I should get a coat A tux or put my order for one. He called they told him come in get fitted then we know what you need Bob went to tux store got fitted then asked when do I come for the tux they told him the day before church.

They told him they will have the tux ready for you because you came in. While out he went to the Mall then walked around to see if anything he would need. He met some of the high school team said hello who is going to coach us my wife will she knows how I coached knows the team. They talked awhile then said see you take care. Bob went home decided to set goals for the baseball team they play 30 games lost four last year. Bob set a goal of 28 wins. Bob was starting to back in a good mood as he Is now setting goals feeling sure about himself. The days went by now the weekend here Caitlin Will be her tonight at 6pm we will go out to a movie also eat out. Bob showered dressed then waited For Caitlin his love.

The bell rung at 6pm Bob opened the door it was Caitlin come in they kissed and sat down Bob asked were will we go tonight. Caitlin said there is a good movie to see Bob said fine lets look in paper for what time. Caitlin said the teachers raved about Lincoln movie. the pitcher starts at 7pm. Bob tells her lets leave. They got to the show before it went on they both enjoyed after the movie they went to dinner at a place they have not been. Bob said the meal is tasty what do you think. Caitlin said this is a new place opened just 6months the meal is good. Bob tells her he got fitted for Tux that it will be ready for him. Caitlin said yes I have to look for a white dress soon.

Caitlin then said teachers are giving me a shower in two weeks at our house. Bob said good I will go out for the day Caitlin said you do not have to leave, go on the patio read a book. Bob said that is an option. Bob said I was at the mall met some of the baseball players. They asked who will coach us. I told them my wife will.

She knows the team also knows who to pitch that she will talk to me to get advice. The team will be ok.

One good thing the college team is there I will coach not build a team like I did with you guys. Yes I will Look to build on it make it better. I just made goals for the team to win 28 games. I will see you take care.

Caitlin said to Bob should she make goals for high school team. Bob said if you want to do it. Do it with your team involve them. You saw how I worked the pitchers do the same thing. Caitlin said I better go it is late. They kissed then she left for home. Bob got a book went to bed to read. At 11:30pm put book down and went to sleep. The next day Sunday bob took it easy then watched a baseball game at 2pm. At 4:30pm he got a dinner out of freezer put in microwave. When it was ready he had a soda with it watched tv till 10pm.

Went to bed Monday he starts college teaching. Monday came Bob up at 6am got dressed ate went to college.

At the college personal dept had him fill out some papers then showed him his room. When the class came in. he introduced himself said first time teaching co-ed. Get your history books out to page 10. We will go over pages 10 to 20 this morning. Bob then talked to them about what those pages had to say then added his take about what they were trying to do or say. When the bell rung for lunch Bob said today I want the girls to eat with me the boys tomorrow. At lunch he asked them I f any of them involved with sports. Five raised hands Bob asked what sports. Three were volley ball two track long distance runners. Bob said that was good. I feel that sports open doors for you. The afternoon class went over pages 21 to 40. Bob said study tonight.

Bob then said because I will test you on what we talked about today. At 3pm the bell rings class leaves Bob then goes to his baseball office. The other coach was there with his son introduced him to Bob You're a big boy what position do you play. He said catcher mostly. Bob said we need a catcher so come To practice Tuesday. Bob asked coach you said we have a bus for away games that holds cheer leaders.

Plus band. The coach said yes plus our players and equipment. Bob said ok that is good. My last team Had no band come with us. We had team then plenty of people. The son said my father said you team Did not lose a game including the district game. Bob said yes plus I built the team.

This team here was as started by your father I will build on it as we go. Already I got two players coming here the top pitcher shortstop who were a big factor in our wins. Adding you as well will make team very good. I put a goal of 28 wins first year. Baseball starts here march so we got a little time to know each other. I got a big day coming up Sept first week Saturday getting married.

The coach said to who Caitlin she graduated here she Is physical dept teacher. She will also coach the high school team next year. She coached with me last year. I recommended her to principle. Bob then said I will go home now but expect you at field on Tuesday. The catcher said ill be there. When Bob got home Caitlin came they talked about the wedding everything seemed to be going right. Caitlin asked him how he felt teaching a co-ed class. Bob said nothing unuseable I just went with they wanted me to teach added myself in like I do most times. The class is smart one right now.

Caitlin said how are the girls behaving. I met with them fore lunch asked them questions to get to know them.

I did the same with the boys the next day. I asked the boys anybody play baseball. Two hands went up Bob asked what position who did you play for. One pitched for little league the other played outfield in little league. Both boys 6feet 2 inches. Bob said I coach the baseball team here, we have tryouts on Tuesday after class. If you are interested come tryout bring glove. When Tuesday came after 3pm Bob went to field.

Saw the catcher plus the two boys in class. Bob told them to go to mound warm up. Told the catcher To catch them. Bob went to mound to watch how they threw. He also had the other boy go to 2nd base Bob on the fifth pitch called for the catcher to throw to 2nd base. Bob saw a very strong arm from catcher Then had the pitcher throw 10 more. He wanted to see how they hit. He had the pitcher throw batting Practice. Bob caught when the catcher hits. The outfield boy hit the ball well Bob then had him bunt run to first. The catcher up he hit very well also putting one over the fence in left. Bob asked him who did you play for he said the high school nothing since.

I just did not think about it till my dad told me about you. Bob said you have a strong arm to second base then you hit the ball well. I will teach you game calling You're my catcher this next season. To the pitcher said you're my next pitcher to watch more. The outfielder he said you can run fast hit good you're my center fielder. The baseball team lost some players So you will play. Bob then said lets rap it up see you in class Wednesday. Bob thinking to himself thought A great find in catcher. A good pitcher third or fourth. Outfielder fast who can catch plus hit. I must be Dreaming. Bob went home ate then took his book out to patio went to lounger to read. About 7pm the Front door bell rung Bob answered the door it was Caitlin hi she said Bob kissed her said hi.

Bob told her About Tue practice how amazed he was to find three players for team. Caitlin said you are a magnet to get Ball players. Bob said the catcher strong arm hit ball over left field fence he is the other coaches son. The other two boys are in my class. A pitcher also outfielder. College team will be a very strong team. Caitlin said you're a great manager of people. Bob said thanks I take it very serious plus I want to win. Caitlin said College ball has very strong teams I saw them when I went to their games while there.

The pitching is better Bob said your right but our team is getting good players added to replace those who left. All colleges have the same problem but can they replace their team with good players. Caitlin said my be your right. Bob said come here next to me for awhile. They kissed then watched a news program. After Caitlin left. Bob went to bed with a book. At 11pm he put book away went to sleep. The wedding cards went out the time went by it was one week to wedding. Bob in class Monday continued on with history teaching when day ended class left Bob was at his desk grading a test he gave them. His test was ten questions on what they went over Tuesday. Bob knows he has a good class the test proves it everyone got 100 percent.

Bob told the personal dept about his wedding Saturday months ago. The replies were coming in the estimate about 50 people. The time moved on it was Friday Bob has to pick up parents sister at 5pm.

He went to airport saw normal time for arrival. The time was 4:30 pm Bob waited at the gate for them when the plain arrived Bob saw his parents sister they saw him waved they all kissed each other. Bob said lets go to luggage. After putting the luggage in the trunk they left to Bobs house. When they got there they all helped with the luggage. Bob said to parents take my bedroom get settled in. To sister he said there is a couch bed in my office take that for the stay. They kissed Bob left her there to settle in. Bob ordered a pizza pie with some chicken wings when it arrived they all ate talked about how cute his home was. Let meshow you the back yard patio. They all liked it said it's a big yard. Bob said I come out here to read books.

We also had a barbeque for the baseball team. They stayed out there talking about everything Bob said I just took the teaching coaching job at Iowa college. My income doubled to 64,000 my girl does not have to work when have a child. The phone rang it was Caitlin asked Bob bring everyone to my home meet aunt plus me. Bob said to family lets take a ride meet my girl. They got in car went to Caitlin home was greeted by Caitlin the mother said she is a beautiful girl. Bob said she lost her parents when she was 14 years old they were killed in a head on crash. That is terrible news Bob said her aunt took her in raised her since.

The mother put her arm around Caitlin said Bob told me about your parents that was tragic. Caitlin saw how nice his parents were. The aunt said I made coffee have some crackers also. While they all drank their coffee the mother said so you took Caitlin in yes she said my sister died in that crash I had too.

After coffee it got late Bob said we better go we got to get up early it is a big day. They all kissed goodbye Bobs mother hugged Caitlin said now you have a big family. Bob drove home they all went to bed. The The next day came Bob was up at 6am he showered then ate then put on his tux. Everyone was up by 8am got showered dressed saw Bob in his tux his mother said look dashing. The church is at 10am then The meal at 5pm. Caitlin was up at 7am she showered then put on wedding dress. A car will pick her up Then go to Bobs house. Will fit the whole family. Avery large white Cadillac. It was getting close to 9am All were ready to go.

The car came at 9:?30am took family to church the aunt was taking Caitlin down the isle. The church was ready the organ played here comes the bride they got married. Now back to Bobs home. They all got casual waited till 4pm then headed to the hill place. The mother said very nice place the room was big all setup for wedding complete with band. Ed was there greeted Bob said what time you leaving 7pm Bob said. Ed said I will watch the envelopes for you. Bob said thanks enjoy yourself too. the toast came from Ed the best man he said to two great people I had the privileged to know good health plus enjoy each other have children raise them just like you.

They drank to Ed toast. The band started to play Bob and Caitlin danced then whole floor was filled with guest dancing. They started to serve the tables so When they finished dancing they went to their tables then started to eat. There was soft music while they ate from recordings while band ate after the main meal the band played dance music Bob & Caitlin danced when the desert came they went to table to eat it the wedding cake. Daddies little girl played the aunt danced with Caitlin. Bobs father then danced with Caitlin then Bob for they will leave at 7pm.

It was 6:30pm now. Bob told Ed to get the envelopes together we will leave soon. Bob told the aunt see that Lady in the hallway that is who you pay. Caitlin and I will leave back to my house to change. Bob said on the mike that we appreciate you all continue to enjoy the band Caitlin and I are leaving for honeymoon.

The guest clapped then they leave. Ed gave them the envelopes Bob said to Ed thanks. Ed said safe trip. they got to their home changed to casual clothing then left for airport. At the airport they have time to get to the plane it was 8pm the flight was 10pm. They just relaxed till they boarded the plane to New York.

They arrived at 11:45 pm got their luggage then took a hotel at airport. They were really tired then slept

The next morning up at 8am they called for something to eat. They then ate while going through envelopes

Bob was surprised by what they were given a total of 3700.00 his parents gave them 1,000. Bob said we will have a good time in city. They then left to his parents home got there half hour. Bob said I was raised here this was my room growing up. Bob then said now lets go to the city. They arrived in the city times sq. area parked at the parking garage. Then walked till 2pm then got something to eat. Caitlin said you were not kidding lots people here. They got to ice skating rink took that in then radio musical hall at 2:45pm got tickets to next show. At 4pm. Continued to walk looking at all the show places they have. Saw a play they wanted to see got tickets for the next day at 6pm. Then went back to radio musical hall to see show.

Coming out of show Caitlin said that was great. It was now 6:30 pm looked for a place to eat picked out China eating in place enjoyed the food then went back to garage to go home. They got home at 8:45pm. Put their clothes away then went to living room watched tv for hour went to bed.

The next day they went To statute of liberty Caitlin was very impressed. Then to museum took 2 hours there to see everything. Then to diamond district then to central park walked around had lunch then walked more sat on bench Then headed to show area. Enjoyed a ice cream cone continued walking looking headed to their show.

Gave them the tickets the show began at 4pm ended at 6pm they both enjoyed the show. After show they saw a place to eat had supper there. Bob said lets go home. They got home at 8pm. They relaxed on The couch kissing each other while news program was on. They turned off tv went to bedroom had sex Next day they were off to coney island had lunch at a very popular place walked the boardwalk for hour. Then went to Jans a very popular place had a split ice cream cup. Caitlin enjoyed herself.

Bob then took her to zoo where they saw all animals they had in hand a stick with flower candy which Caitlin enjoyed. Then they went to parade grounds where Bob played ball. Caitlin said they have lots of playing fields here. Bob said they also have plenty of good players played here. They then went to Bobs parents home to relax. Bob said N.Y. A very busy place you can see why I moved to Iowa. Caitlin said yes this city is opened 24 hours a day. They continued there stay until time to go home.

They clean the house they used then headed to airport. Returned the car at the airport then went to their plane back toIowa. They landed fine, Ed picked them up drove them home. When they got there it will be the first night Caitlin stays in the home married to Bob. Ed left Bob thanked him then Caitlin came out to say goodbye Bob picked Caitlin up brought her into the home. Caitlin loves Bob when he put her down told her this is our home now. Bob asked her should he order a pizza Caitlin said yes I am to tired to cook. When the pizza came he open it they both ate it with soda watching tv. News sports.

There was no trades since he left they also watched weather found rain on next day 60 percent. This was Friday ack to class Monday. They talked about children when do you want them. Bob said let it happen I make enough now to handle it. Bob said lets do it now. Off to the bedroom they went had sex they were so in love. Bob tells Caitlin how many children would you like. Caitlin said my be 4 at max. Bob said then we have to go to work each month un till we get 4. Have our children early so we will be still young when they leave the house.

Bob tells Caitlin if we just let it happen we can afford them. The college announced new pay structure for teachers And coaches while Bob was away. With what they give Bob would go from 64,000 to 72,000 total. Bob will learn about this Monday. Saturday came it was raining hard till 2pm when Caitlin looked outside she Saw it stopped. Bob she said yes he said lets go shopping to see what they can offer for children furniture.

We can see that in the mall. Bob said lets go see what they got. They went to mall found store looked at all they had to offer. They were in the store quite a while looking. Bob said lets go we saw what they had.

They left the mall went to her aunts home. The aunt was glad to see them said to Caitlin how did you like New York. Caitlin said the place is great to see so much to see but not for me. I will stay in Iowa. Her aunt Said you both look great had a good time there. Caitlin said I enjoyed it we saw a show there we went to Statue of liberty, central park zoo, museum of natural history, cony island, plus walked times square. It was A big place with very tall buildings open 24 hours it seemed. I had good food and good time. Here is a gift For you taffy its delicious. Are you guys hungry no said Bob we ate before we came here. How about a cup of coffee they said yes. The aunt went to kitchen came out with fresh coffee and cake.

They had it then she Said it is good to see you again. Bob said we have to go because we are tired from the trip. The aunt said I Will see you soon. They left to go home Caitlin said it feels queer to leave her. Bob said I can understand That she was like your mother to you.

Bob then said but now you're my wife, my life I love you. Caitlin Tells Bob I love you too. They get home put on tv to watch the news sports. The yanks did not make the Playoffs they lost several players. The rays made the playoffs will play rangers next week. Toronto also They play braves. Bob then turned off the tv said I am going to read a book. Caitlin said I will clean up Then go to bed. At 10pm she went to bed Bob already put book down fell asleep. The next day Sunday Caitlin made breakfast pancakes Bob got up what is that sweet smell it is pancakes Caitlin says. Bob said you cook as well. Caitlin said my aunt taught me how to cook. I think that is great Bob tells her. Lets see how good it is. Bob had two helpings he was really hungry liked how she made them. Caitlin asked Bob what are we doing today. Bob said take it easy t is back to work Monday. How about a barbeque lunch today love she said sounds good to me.

The back needs mowing I will do that now. Bob got the mower mowed the back yard then put the mower in garage. He washed up then laid in lounger with a book Caitlin said we need some things from the store I will get them now Bob said ok. She left came back with bag full of things put everything away then put on tv watched a movie. Bob was in the lounger reading a book.

About 5pm Bob put book down put on the grill went inside got ribs from the freezer plus corn on cob Bob started to cook Caitlin watching movie was entrenched into it. Bob saw that did not bother her just Cooked the ribs and corn. When it was ready he put it on two plates went to tv room with it put plate in front of Caitlin who was startled for a minute said you cooked already. Bob said yes eat while it is hot.

After they finished eating Bob put coffee on saw Caitlin bought pound cake cut two pieces brought it all in Caitlin took her piece of pound cake ate it sipped coffee as did Bob. When they finished Bob took cups & plates back to kitchen. Bob stayed with Caitlin arms around her watching movie until movie ended then Bob told Caitlin that he was going on patio to read a book. The time was 6:30pm Caitlin went to patio asked him. Does he want to make love. Bob put book down said lets do it, they both went to bedroom enjoyed each other. Caitlin said after awhile Bob what we have to do is make a menu I remember my mother doing that.

We need to do that for dinner only. It is better then putting my hands up as what to make. Bob said my mother did that too. Bob yes he said I think because I am late with my period I might be pregnant. Bob said

Then go to a doctor to find out. Caitlin said I will wait to see if I get my period it might be just late. If not I Will go to doctor. Bob kissed her said I love you she said. I love you to. The days went by back to class at school Bob told class go to page 65 follow me learn what England did to hurt Germany. This class to was smart as well. Germany had a big ship that would bring havoc to the seas. It had to be destroyed that was on Churchill mind. When it was seen England brought all destroyers in area to destroy it they did just that it sunk after taking just to many torpedoes plus being hit by many salvos from destroyers. That hurt Germany when the Japan attacked pearl harbor the United States declared war on Japan Thus entering with England &

France the war on Germany & Japan & Italy. The big forces of these Countries Plus the great manufacturing of the United States ultimately was to much as the war was over after we bombed with atomic bombs on two of Japans cities. The powerful effect was just to much for Japan to take. Many lives were lost many hurt

With the effect of radiation some are living today. Germany surrendered after Hitler died and Russia was Pounding them from the rear. Then the big army of England, USA, invaded France chased Germany out. Saving France from occupation. Then the bombing of Germany they had no choice. The class was into it Asked questions on atomic Bombs the USA used. Bob said it saved lives of our country & England. War Is terrible thousands of lives are lost. The war would have continued several more years. They were trying to win as well. Bob said after Japan bombed pearl harbor our navy sunk Japans 4 destroyers at midway.

Bob said remember we were not the one who started this they were the aggressors. Hitler was trying to be something that Germany got infected with. They gassed thousands of Jew people another story in its self.

As we go through this story remember to read your chapters we went over. There will be a ten question test

Friday what we went over this week. The bell rings for lunch Bob goes to coaches office to eat sandwich with coach. They discussed the team Bob tells coach his goals for baseball team. The bell rings back to class.

The class comes in they go over what they talked about in morning. Bob continues on second world war then tells class to read these chapters we will go over it tomorrow. Time moves now it is thanksgiving time the time was spent at Caitlin aunts home. Then Christmas Bob put up his first tree with Caitlin in living room.

Bob had Christmas dinner at home invited Caitlin aunt to join them. Bob got Caitlin a cross 14 caret necklace. They got Bob a jacket for winter and socks. They got the aunt a sweater then they ate dinner had coffee cake the aunt brought. Bob said the time is moving before we know it June will be here. Caitlin said twenty more weeks. Bob laughed said I love you, Caitlin said I love you. The aunt said I love both of you. The aunt said are you planning anything for New Years. Bob said yes we are taking you to hilltop for dinner with New Years celebration. New Years came the time was 6pm the dinner was for 6pm they sat near the dance floor. The meal was served all ate then continued dancing. To recorded music un till the band started at 8pm they danced with each other, the dance floor was filling up as was the room. When it got to 12pm Bob kissed Caitlin also kissed the aunt. They left at 12:30 because Caitlin was with baby the aunt was tired as well. They dropped off the aunt went home went straight to bed. The next day was Saturday January 1 they got up at 9am had something to eat then relaxed watched tv awhile.

Then Bob mowed the Back yard as Caitlin made bed cleaned the kitchen. They decided to see a early movie home alone playing t the mall movie. After movie ended at 3pm they walked the mall then went home. The time moved then June came Caitlin had baby boy at 6lbs 3 ounces. Bob was starting practice for college they all were happy With son as he grew. Bob took college team to goal of 28 wins 2 losses won title. Caitlin stayed at home Raising son. The high school team repeated title with 27 wins 3 losses. Their son Jason was their joy.

The college coach left with his wife to florida. His son the catcher had a great season hitting 285 10 home Runs, 72 runs batted in. Bob thinks he could be drafted first round. The college liked his coaching Bob Thought life was great it could not be better then fulfilling a teachers dream.

The End